ISBN-13: 978-0-439-90652-4
ISBN-10: 0-439-90652-0

Copyright © 2004 by Eileen Christelow. All rights reserved. Published by Scholastic Inc., 557 Broadway, New York, NY 10012, by arrangement with Clarion Books, a Houghton Mifflin Company imprint. SCHOLASTIC and associated logos are trademarks and/or registered trademarks of Scholastic Inc.

12 11 10 9 8 7 6 5 4 3 2 1   6 7 8 9 10 11/0

Printed in Mexico   49

First Scholastic printing, October 2006

The illustrations were executed in pen and ink and acrylic gouache.

The text was set in 19-point Weiss.

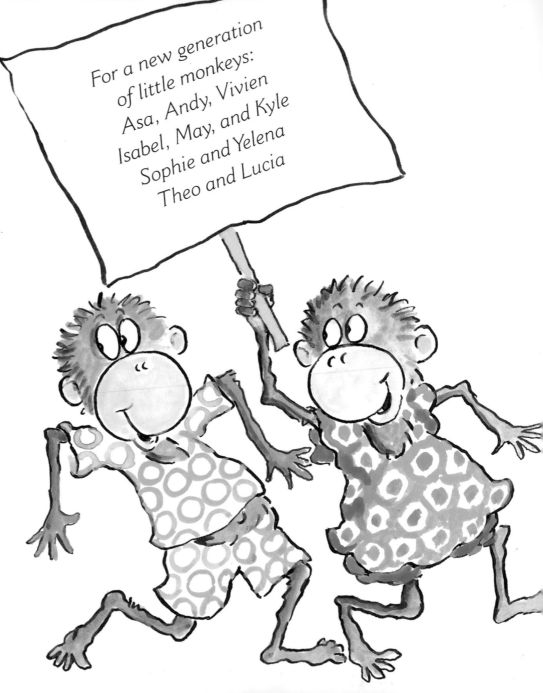

For a new generation
of little monkeys:
Asa, Andy, Vivien
Isabel, May, and Kyle
Sophie and Yelena
Theo and Lucia

FIVE Little MONKEYS
play hide-and-seek

SCHOLASTIC INC.
New York   Toronto   London   Auckland   Sydney
Mexico City   New Delhi   Hong Kong   Buenos Aires

The five little monkeys
are ready for bed.
Their mama's going dancing.
She's dressed in bright red.

"Lulu's the sitter.
You'd better be good.
No tricks! No silliness!
Is that understood?"

3

"We'll be good!" shout the monkeys.
"We'll play hide-and-seek!
 Hey, Lulu, you're it!
 And you'd better not peek!"

"Just one game," says Lulu.
"Then it's right off to bed.
Your bedtime's at eight.
That's what your mama said."

Lulu starts counting.
She counts up to ten.

1 2 3 4

"Where are those monkeys?
Where did they go?
Where are they hiding?
I really don't know!"

But wait! . . .
"I see some fingers.
I see some toes.
I see some eyes.
I see a nose."

9

"No fair!" shout the monkeys.
"You found us too fast!
Let's play one more game.
And this will be the last!"

"Hold on!" says Lulu.
"It's time for bed.
'No tricks! No silliness!'
That's what your mama said."

"Oh, *please,*" say the monkeys.
"Just one game more?
And this time can you count
to at least twenty-four?"

"Okay," sighs Lulu.
  She's counted to four
  when those monkeys start sneaking
  right out the front door.

13

"Where are those monkeys?
Where did they go?
Where are they hiding?
I really don't know!"

But wait. . .
"I see some fingers.
I see some toes.
I see some eyes.
I see a nose!"

"No fair!" shout the monkeys.
"You found us too fast!
  Let's play another game.
  And this will be the last."

"Hold on!" says Lulu.
"It's past time for bed.
'No tricks! No silliness!'
That's what your mama said."

19

But the monkeys convince her
to play one game more,
and Lulu starts counting
to one hundred and four.

1 2 3 4 5 6 7 8 9 10 11 12 13 14 15 16 17 18 19 20 21 22 23 24 25 26

29 30 31 32 33 34 35 36 37 38 39 40 41 42 43 44 45 46 47 48 49 50 51...

"Quick!" shout the monkeys.
"We all need to hide
in a place she won't think of
—somewhere inside."

21

...52 53 54 55 **56** 57 58 59 **60** 61 62 63 64 65 66 67 68 69 70 71 72

"Let's hide in the closet!"
"No, behind the chair!"
"No, under this table!"
"But she'll find us there!"

"Wait!" says one monkey.
She heads for the hall.
"I know a place
she won't think of at all!"

23

Lulu stops counting.
She looks all around.
"Where are those monkeys?"
There isn't a sound!

She looks behind bushes.

She searches the tree.

She hunts in the closets.

Where can they be?

Under the table?
Behind the big chair?
Those five little monkeys
aren't anywhere!

27

"Come on, you monkeys!
  It's past time for bed.
  'No tricks! No silliness!'
  That's what your mama said."

Lulu is worried.
"Where *can* they be?
  They'll never get to bed,
  and their mama will blame me!"

Just then, in comes Mama.
"Did the children behave?"
"They're gone!" Lulu wails.
She tries to be brave.

"Gone?" says Mama.
She scratches her head.
"I just peeked in their window,
and saw them in . . .

"We fooled you!"
   shout the monkeys.
"Now, let's play again.
   Lulu, *you* hide,
   and *we'll* count to ten."

"No way!" says Lulu.
"You've got to go to sleep.
   But if you want to count,
   I'll help you count . . .

. . . SHEEP!"

And so they start counting.
They're up to thirty-four,
when those five little monkeys
all start to snore.